BOARD BATTLE

SPORT STORIES

TEXT BY ERIC STEVENS
ILLUSTRATED BY ABURTOV

raintree

a Capstone company — publishers for children

Raintree is an imprint of Capstone Global Library Limited, a company
incorporated in England and Wales having its registered office at 264 Banbury
Road, Oxford, OX2 7DY – Registered company number: 6695582

www.raintree.co.uk
myorders@raintree.co.uk

Designed by Veronica Scott
Original illustrations © Capstone Global Library Limited 2018
Illustrated by Aburtov
Production by Tori Abraham
Originated by Capstone Global Library Limited
Printed and bound in China

ISBN 978 1 4747 3238 3
21 20 19 18 17
10 9 8 7 6 5 4 3 2 1

British Library Cataloguing in Publication Data
A full catalogue record for this book is available from the British Library.

CONTENTS

CHAPTER 1

NEW KIDS

Conner Klout was on his back. He could hear his skateboard rolling back and forth along the bottom of the half-pipe next to him.

"Fail!" his friend Hannah Lowery shouted. She stood at the top of the half-pipe, three metres above him.

Conner waited for his board to roll to a stop against his thigh. Then he grabbed it and sat up.

"You have to admit," he said, "I came pretty close that time."

"Close to a concussion?" Hannah replied with a smirk.

"Very funny," Conner said, climbing to his feet.

"Watch out," Hannah said. "I'll show you how it's done."

Conner dropped his board and rolled off the half-pipe to make room for Hannah. Before he'd even turned to watch, Hannah dropped in. She took a few passes back and forth to pick up speed.

On the third pass, Hannah got some air off the far side of the pipe. She flew straight up from the ramp, pulled up her knees, grabbed her skateboard and spun around completely. A perfect Indy 360.

"Yes!" Conner shouted.

For pros, an Indy 360 was a basic trick. But for Conner and Hannah, it was a big deal. Conner still couldn't do it, which is why he had ended up flat on his back at the bottom of the ramp at the end of his turn.

Hannah took another pass and then rolled to a stop at the bottom. She pulled off her helmet, and Conner gave her a high five.

"Not bad, huh?" Hannah said.

"Amazing," Conner said. He wasn't ashamed to admit that Hannah was better than he was on the half-pipe. "I'll get it eventually, though."

"Definitely," Hannah agreed. "And for now, you wreck me on the street course anyway."

Slim's Skate Park, the only indoor skate park in Hilltop, had a full street course. Hannah and Conner had raced through it many times, and Conner always won. The park also had lots of ramps of different sizes. It only had one half-pipe, though.

The park opened at 8 am on Saturdays, and Conner and Hannah were always the first ones there. Usually no one else showed up until lunchtime.

"I'm going to take another shot at it," Conner said. He stood up and hopped onto the bottom of the ramp.

"Watch out, newbie," called a voice from the top.

Conner squinted up the pipe. The bright lights mounted on the high ceiling shined in his eyes.

"Where'd you come from?" Hannah said, glaring up at the top of the ramp.

Conner shaded his eyes. A big guy, not much older than they were, stood at the top of the ramp, ready to drop in.

"Doesn't matter," the boy said. "Tell your friend to snap out of it and get out of my way before I run him over." Without waiting for a response, he dropped in.

Conner hurried off the ramp and stood next to Hannah. Two other boys came up behind them.

"Watch this," one of them said. "Hank will show you what good skating really is."

The other boy laughed as Hank picked up some speed on the pipe. "Yeah," he said. "We really enjoyed watching you two celebrate that lame Indy."

Both boys cracked up as Hank started his tricks on the pipe. He did an Indy 360 easily. On the next pass he added a rotation to make it a 540 and did the next pass backwards.

After he had picked up some speed, Hank went for the big one – a 720. He landed it easily. Behind Conner and Hannah, his friends cheered and shouted.

Even Conner clapped. *He's really good*, he thought. *Even if his friends are a bit annoying.*

Hank rolled off the ramp and came to a stop in front of them.

"That was really great," Hannah said. "I've never seen you at the park before, though. Have you just moved here or something?"

Hank grinned at her, but he didn't answer. He just stood there with his hands on his hips and looked back and forth from Hannah to Conner.

"Yeah," Conner said, trying to break the silence. "Really impressive. I can't even pull off that 360 yet."

Hank stepped aside. "Take your turn," he said. "Drew, Jay and I want to skate."

Conner stepped onto his board to enter the pipe. Just as his foot hit the skateboard, Hank took a menacing step towards him, like he was going to knock him off.

Conner flinched. His board shot out from under him, and he fell to the floor.

"Wow," said Hank as his friends laughed at Conner on the floor. "I wasn't going to hit you, idiot."

Conner looked up at Hank, but he didn't say anything.

"That was mean," Hannah said. She helped Conner to his feet.

"Whatever," Hank said. He turned to his friends. "Let's run the street course until the babies have finished with the half-pipe."

Hannah crossed her arms and stared at Conner as Hank, Drew and Jay rolled off.

"What?" Conner said.

"I can't believe you let him do that!" Hannah said.

"What was I supposed to do?" Conner said. "Fight him? He's huge! Anyway, I didn't come here to fight. I came here to skate."

"So you're just going to let him get away with it?" Hannah said.

Conner watched as Hank started running the street course. The big new kid did a grind across a rail followed by a kick-flip. Then he turned and coasted up and over some ramps.

"You're really not going to do anything?" Hannah asked.

Conner took a deep breath and shook his head. "No way," he said.

CHAPTER 2

CLOSE CALL

The following Saturday, Conner and Hannah were back at Slim's. They were only on the half-pipe for fifteen minutes before the three new kids slammed through the skate park's heavy double doors.

"Those three boys are back," Hannah warned. "And they're coming over here."

Conner stood at the top of the pipe next to Hannah and watched Hank, Drew and Jay stomp towards them.

"I bet they'll try to kick us off the half-pipe," Hannah said. "They're such bullies."

But when the three boys reached the pipe, Hank just stood at the bottom with his fists on his hips. "Well, come on," he said, looking irritated. "We're not going to wait all day. Hurry up and take your turn so I can go."

Hannah glanced and shrugged. "You go first," she said.

Conner nodded and dropped in. He picked up speed and went up the far side. At the top, he let his board come back down and picked up more speed on the way back.

When he crossed the pipe again, he was going fast enough to clear the lip just a tiny bit. Then, on his next pass, he was really zooming. He decided to go for the 360.

But as Conner crossed the bottom of the ramp at top speed, he spotted Hank out of the corner of his eye. The new boy's helmet was off, and he threw it across the floor of the half-pipe.

Conner watched the helmet roll into his path. He struggled to control his board and just managed to miss crashing into the helmet. But the trick was blown, and Conner lost his balance. To avoid a wipeout, he dropped from the board onto his knee pads and slid to a stop.

For a second, the whole park fell silent.

"Are you crazy?" Hannah shouted from the top of the ramp. She stuck her board under her arm and slid to the bottom of the half-pipe on her knees. Then she jumped to her feet and got right up next to Hank, holding her board like a weapon.

"Whoa!" Conner said. He grabbed Hannah's shoulders and pulled her away from the bully. "Calm down!"

Hank and his friends, who had looked terrified for a moment, started laughing.

"Yeah, you'd better hold back your girlfriend, newbie," Hank said. "She's going to get herself in trouble with that temper."

"I'm not his girlfriend!" Hannah snapped, pulling away from Conner's grip. "And what you did was really stupid. Conner could have been seriously hurt."

"He's fine," Hank said. "Now are you going to take a turn, or are you going to back off so we can finally use the pipe?"

Hannah glared at Hank for a moment. Then she threw her board to the floor and skated off.

"Wait!" Conner shouted. He had to hurry to catch her before she left the park. "Where are you going?"

"I don't know," Hannah said. Her face was red. Conner didn't know if she was about to cry or scream in anger.

"You weren't really going to hit someone with your board, Hannah," Conner said. "Were you?"

"I don't think so," she said. "But what are we supposed to do? Just put up with them?"

Conner turned around and watched one of Hank's friends on the pipe. He was good, but not as good as Hank.

"I don't know," Conner said. "We'll find somewhere else to skate."

CHAPTER 3

THE OLD PARK

An hour later, Conner and Hannah were across town at the old outdoor skate park. Hannah leaned against the chain-link fence surrounding the park and shook her head.

"I don't like this park," she said.

"Why not?" Conner asked. "It was good enough before Slim's opened. It'll be good enough for us."

Hannah sighed. "Fine. We'll try it," she said.

Hannah dropped her board and pushed into the park to start the street course. But her wheels caught a chunk of cement on the first ramp. The board stopped, and Hannah kept going. She fell flat on her face.

Hannah groaned and climbed to her feet. "This is not working for me," she said, rubbing the scratches on her cheek.

"Think of it as a challenge," Conner said. "It'll make us better skaters."

Conner skated towards the first rail and went for the grind. As soon as his board hit it, though, the rail pulled away from its anchors in the concrete. The railing and Conner both slammed into the ground.

Conner rolled onto his back, holding his left shoulder with his right hand. He gritted his teeth against the pain.

"Are you okay?" Hannah shouted, running to his side.

"I'm fine," Conner grunted. "It hurt, but it's not serious."

"This isn't working, Con," Hannah said. "This park isn't used for a reason. It's falling apart. Let's go back to Slim's. We can't just let them bully us out of there."

"I know," Conner said. He climbed to his feet, wincing at the pain in his sore shoulder. "But I'm not going to fight anyone."

"I respect that," Hannah said as they skated out of the rundown park. "But we have to draw the line somewhere."

Conner knew she was right. He just didn't know how to draw the line.

CHAPTER 4

SLIM'S GAMES

The next Saturday, Hannah and Conner were at Slim's before Slim had even arrived.

"You two are certainly committed," Slim said as he walked up to the front doors.

"We just want to get better," Conner said.

Slim fumbled with his coffee cup and keys. After a few moments, he got the doors unlocked and pushed them open. "Well then, I hope you'll both enter Slim's Games next month," he said, heading to his office.

"I forgot about that," Conner said as he and Hannah headed for the half-pipe. "Are you going to enter? I bet you'd have a shot in our age group on the half-pipe."

"Correction," Hannah said, pulling on her helmet. "I would have had a shot if Hank hadn't shown up. He's got it locked."

Conner sighed. "And his friends are pretty good too," he said.

Hannah nodded and rolled onto the ramp. Then she kicked off, rolling up one side to pick up speed.

"Whoa, whoa!" a voice echoed through the high ceilings of the park.

Conner didn't have to turn around to know Hank and his friends had arrived. Conner looked at Hannah, who'd stopped at the top of the pipe to glare at them.

"I thought we'd worked this out last Saturday," Hank said as he reached the pipe. "When we're here, you two are not."

"You thought wrong," Hannah snapped.

"Come on," said Conner. "We're not bothering anyone."

Hank's friends laughed. "Come on," Drew repeated in a whiny, mocking voice. Then he gave Conner a shove.

Conner put his hands up and backed away. "Come on, Hannah," he said. "Let's just go and practise on the street course."

Hannah growled in frustration. "Fine," she snapped. "Let's go."

She dropped into the pipe and skated right off it, towards the street course. Conner stepped onto his board and followed her.

Hannah stopped at the start of the street course and stepped on her board. She grabbed the nose and banged it on a rail.

"Calm down," Conner said quietly when he reached her. He pointed towards Slim, who was watching them from across the park.

"Whatever," Hannah muttered under her breath. "If anyone gets in trouble here, it should be those guys."

"I know," said Conner.

Hannah sighed. "Let's just practise, okay?" she said.

CHAPTER 5

PUSHED AROUND

Hannah and Conner hadn't been skating for long before Hank and his friends rolled over from the half-pipe.

"Okay, nerds," Hank said as he stopped and flipped his board into his hand. "Time for you to go back to the half-pipe. We want to practise on the street course now."

Conner forced himself to relax and smile. "We've almost finished," he said. "We'll be out of your way in ten minutes."

Hannah's eyes went wide. She looked at Conner. He raised his eyebrows at her.

It might work, he thought.

But it didn't.

Hank's obnoxious grin turned into a frown. "Maybe I wasn't clear," he said, getting right in Conner's face. "It's time for you two to leave the street course. Right now."

Hank put a hand on Conner's chest and gave him a light shove. Conner didn't fall, but he did back off.

"Let's just go, Han," Conner said as he skated off.

Hannah skated up alongside him. "Are you kidding?" she said in an urgent whisper. "You're really just going to let that idiot push you around?"

"I'm not going to get into a fight over it," Conner said. "It's not worth it."

As they reached the half-pipe, Conner heard wheels rolling up behind them. He turned around and saw Jay coming towards them.

"Hey," he said. "I'm sorry."

Conner glanced at Hannah. Her mouth dropped open in shock.

"It's okay," Conner said. "I guess Hank's just kind of –"

But the other boy cut him off. "Sorry because I decided I need some more time on the pipe," he finished.

With a mean grin on his face, Jay pushed off his board and skated right between Hannah and Conner, knocking them both out of the way.

"That's it," Hannah said. She flipped up her board and ran at the boy, holding the board over her head like a giant sword.

"Wait!" Conner called after her. But before he could do anything, Slim ran over.

"Hold it!" he shouted. He grabbed Hannah's board. "Are you insane?"

"But –" Hannah started to say.

Slim wouldn't let her finish. "Out," he said, pointing at the exit. "Come back when you've calmed down."

Hannah glared at him, stomped one foot, and then skated at top speed towards the exit.

"She's having a bad day," Conner said, trying to explain. He glared at Hank's friend and hurried after Hannah. They got to the doors at the same time.

"Leave me alone," Hannah said.

"No way," said Conner. "Slim will get over it."

"It's not fair!" Hannah said. She spun around to face Conner as they reached the pavement outside. "Those boys treat us like that, and I'm the one who gets into trouble?"

"I know," Conner said. "It's not fair."

Just then, a big black car pulled up to the kerb. The window rolled down, and the driver leaned over.

"Hello," he said, looking right at Conner. "Is Hank Redwing in there?"

"Hank?" Conner said. "Yeah. I think so."

"Tell him to get out here right now," the man snapped, rolling the window up.

Just then, the doors slammed open and Hank and his friends came out, laughing and shouting. They shoved past Conner and Hannah and climbed into the car. Hank got into the front passenger seat.

"You're late," the driver snapped as the door slammed shut. "I told you I didn't want to wait for you."

"Sorry," Hank said quietly. Then the car drove off.

"They've gone now," Conner said. "We have the place to ourselves again."

Hannah checked the time on her phone. "It's 9:30 am," she said. "Maybe they finish at this time every Saturday."

They headed back inside, and Hannah went right up to Slim's desk. "Sorry," she said. "I'm calm now."

"I see that," said Slim. "Is that because Hank, Drew and Jay have left?"

Hannah shrugged. "That might have something to do with it," she admitted.

Slim leaned back on his stool and crossed his arms over his stomach.

"We also want to sign up for the competition," Conner said. "Hannah's going to kill it on the half-pipe."

"Conner!" Hannah said, shooting him a look. "He's just joking."

Slim reached under the counter and came back up with his clipboard. "I was wondering when you'd sign up," he said. "You're one of the best kids at the park."

Hannah shrugged, but Conner could tell she was pleased. Her cheeks went a bit red.

Then Slim grabbed a second clipboard and put it in front of Conner. "And here's one for you, Conner," he said.

The words "Street Race Sign-Up Sheet" were written at the top of that paper. Conner took a deep breath and wrote his name on the list.

"This is how we'll fight," Conner said as he and Hannah walked away from the front desk. "No fists. No swinging skateboards."

"Okay," said Hannah. "We'll show them on our boards."

CHAPTER 6

THE PLAN TO PRACTISE

The following Saturday, Conner rode up to Slim's at 9:15 am. Hannah was already there, crouched down behind an overgrown hedge near the fence of the office building next door.

"What are you doing?" Conner asked as he rolled up next to her.

"Shh," said Hannah. She grabbed Conner by the sleeve and pulled him down next to her. "I'm waiting for the car."

"Which car?" Conner asked.

"Keep your voice down!" Hannah hissed.

"I don't think anyone can hear us from here, Han," Conner said.

"Hank's dad's car," Hannah said with a sigh. "We're waiting for those bullies to leave, and when Hank's dad's car gets here, it means they're leaving."

"Or we could go inside," Conner said.

Hannah ignored him. Suddenly, a loud rumble filled the air.

"Here it comes!" Hannah said. She dropped even lower to the ground.

A horn honked loudly, and the heavy doors of the skate park banged open.

"Okay, okay!" Hank shouted as he and his friends stepped outside.

"Watch your tone," the driver snapped. The boys climbed in. Three doors slammed, and the car tyres squealled as it sped off.

Hannah looked up at Conner. "Now it's our turn," she said.

* * *

When they got inside, Hannah went straight to the half-pipe. Conner stood at the start of the street course to watch.

Hannah climbed the steps to the top and took a deep breath. After a quick nod in Conner's direction, she dropped in. On her first pass, she already had enough speed for a quick handplant with a frontside rotation.

"Nice one," Slim said quietly from the desk. Conner could hear him, but he was pretty sure Hannah couldn't as she was all the way across the park.

Conner watched Hannah do one more trick – another perfect Indy 360 – before starting his own practising on the street course.

He pushed off hard to get up some speed before the first small ramp. He kicked his board up to the low rail and grinded it across the platform. Then he landed, ollied and pushed off again.

Conner kick-flipped to the little quarter-pipe, pushed off hard and grabbed some air off the lip of the pipe. But as he landed, the board slipped out from under him. Conner managed to catch himself, but the board shot across the street course and crashed into the flat end of a double-sided ramp.

He looked at Slim and shrugged. "Oops," Conner said.

Slim just shook his head and went back to reading his magazine.

Conner retrieved his board and got right back on the course. He and Hannah spent the whole day at Slim's, only stopping for lunch.

By the time they headed home, Conner was exhausted. *But it'll be worth it*, he thought. *Even if I don't plan to fight with my fists or my skateboard, I still plan to win.*

CHAPTER 7

THE GAMES BEGIN

For the next three weeks, Conner and Hannah practised every Saturday morning as soon as Hank's dad's car drove off. By the time the tournament came around, Conner was in the best skating shape of his life.

The morning of the competition, Hannah's dad gave them a lift to Slim's.

"You two wouldn't want to wear yourselves out on the trip over here, would you?" her dad said on the drive there.

"Thanks, Dad," said Hannah.

Conner stared out of the back window as they headed across town. The car zipped past the old, rundown skate park.

"Hey, Hannah," Conner said. He nodded towards the old park. "Shall we do some practice on the way there?"

Hannah laughed and shook her head. "Never again," she said.

Conner smiled. *Maybe if we do well enough in Slim's Games, we'll have our park back*, he thought.

* * *

When they arrived, Slim's was more crowded than Conner had ever seen it. It got crowded sometimes on Saturdays and after school, but this was different.

Conner recognized a few kids from school and plenty of kids he'd seen around the park occasionally. But most of the people wandering around the skate park weren't wearing numbers for the tournament.

They must just be here to watch, Conner realized.

There were lots of other kids with numbers pinned onto the backs of their T-shirts, though. Conner hardly recognized any of them.

"There must be people here from all over the city," Hannah whispered, sounding a little bit nervous.

At the same time, Hannah and Conner spotted Hank's father walking through the big double doors. Hank, Drew and Jay were right behind him.

Hannah smiled and narrowed her eyes. She rubbed her hands together. "Excellent," she said.

"Whoa," said Conner with a grin. "You're quite scary right now, you know that?"

"Good," Hannah said as Slim picked up the microphone. "Wait till you see me on the half-pipe."

"Welcome, everyone," Slim's voice boomed through the speaker system. "Attention please, all skaters. And quiet from the crowd, please?"

After several moments of clapping and cheering from the crowd, the park settled down.

"We're about to begin the first ever Slim's Games!" Slim shouted.

The park went wild with cheering again. When everyone finally calmed down, Slim announced, "The first event will be the middle school half-pipe competition."

"Looks like you're up before me," Conner said. Hannah's smile grew even bigger.

CHAPTER 8

THE HALF-PIPE

Hannah was up third out of the six half-pipe competitors. When it was her turn, she climbed the steps to the top of the pipe. At the lip, she leaned back on the tail of her board so the rest of it stuck out over the ramp. Then she dropped in.

Hannah's first trick was her perfect Indy 360. On the next pass, she grinded both trucks from one side of the lip to the other, and then finished with a 180 off the lip.

"Nice one, Han!" Conner cheered from the stands. He spotted Hank on the other side of the pipe, waiting for his turn. The bully glared at him.

Hannah finished up the first of her two thirty-second runs on the half-pipe with a long handplant and grab. She stayed suspended on the lip for the final few seconds of her run. The crowd went mad.

When the buzzer sounded, Conner hurried over to meet her. "That handstand was amazing!" he said. "When did you practise that?"

"When do you think?" Hannah said, smiling. "The past couple of weeks while you were on the street course."

They both watched Slim to see how she'd done. He held up a score of eight.

"Yes!" Hannah said, pumping her fist.

Hank's friend Drew was up next.

"Isn't Hank doing this event?" Conner asked.

Hannah shrugged. "I suppose not," she said.

They watched as Drew dropped into the half-pipe. He was good – but not as good as Hank. Even still, he pulled off a perfect 540 rotation. Conner noticed Hannah's smile faded a little when he did.

"You were just as good as he is," Conner said. "One trick doesn't matter."

"Maybe," said Hannah.

Then Slim held up Drew's score of nine, and Hannah looked even more worried than before.

Hannah's second turn on the half-pipe was just as strong as her first – until the very end. She went for the 540 air. She missed the full turn, though, and her board got away from her. She slid down the ramp on her back and rolled onto her stomach.

The crowd gasped and then went silent.

"Hannah!" Conner shouted. "Are you okay?"

Hannah nodded and climbed to her knees as the timer ran out. The crowd cheered. Slim put up her score: seven.

Conner felt an elbow in his side. "Ow," he said, turning. Hank stood next to him, snarling.

"Your girlfriend blew it," Hank said. "And now you're about to blow it on the street course. Against me."

CHAPTER 9

STREET COURSE

On the street course, each skater got one ninety-second run. Slim would judge the run based on how many tricks the skater performed, how well the skater did and how much of the course was used.

Conner recognized the first skater on the street course. He'd seen him sometimes around Slim's after school. His run was pretty good, but Conner knew his real competition would be Hank.

Hank's run was aggressive and intense. His grinds were extreme. His trucks slapped against the rails and squealled loudly. He moved quickly from box to ramp to rail. At the end of his turn, Hank did a 360 grab off the biggest ramp. His time ran out just as he stuck the landing.

Slim held up his score: nine.

"You'll never beat that," Hank said confidently as he skated past Conner.

Conner was up next. He clicked the chin strap of his helmet and gave Hannah a high five. Then he hit the course.

After weeks of practising, Conner's body seemed to move on its own. He pushed off and glided to the first low rail. He ollied to a backside 50-50. Back on the ground, he kick-flipped to the two-sided ramp.

Up one side, Conner got enough air to clear the flat top of the ramps. He pulled up his knees in mid-air and grabbed the board. Then he landed on the other side and shot to the quarter-pipe.

Conner was flying. He had enough speed and air to go for a 360. It wasn't part of the routine that he'd practised, but he really wanted to win. He wanted his skate park back.

I'm going for it, Conner thought. *I know I can do this.*

But out of the corner of his eye, Conner caught a glimpse of Hank. The bully stood off to the side of the street course, right next to the quarter-pipe.

What's he doing? Conner thought. *He shouldn't be standing so close.*

Suddenly Conner realized what Hank was up to. The bully had shoved his board with his foot, right across the top of the quarter-pipe – and it was coming straight for Conner.

CHAPTER 10

EJECTED!

Whistles suddenly blew loudly, and Slim's voice screamed over the speaker system.

Conner tried to turn at the last instant, but his board collided with Hank's. Conner landed on his back on the quarter-pipe and slid to the bottom.

"Ungggh . . ." Conner muttered as he rolled onto his stomach. He heard footsteps running towards him. They were Hannah's.

"Are you okay?" Hannah asked.

Conner nodded and muttered, "Yeah, I think so."

"You're out of here, Hank," Slim said. Conner saw the big park owner standing over him. He didn't look happy.

"It was an accident," Hank said, rolling his eyes.

Conner got up on his knees. "No, it wasn't," he said, staring right at Hank. "You pushed your board with your foot. I saw it."

Hank's dad pushed through the crowd and grabbed his son by the elbow.

"Is that true?" the man demanded angrily.

"No, Dad," Hank said. He pulled his arm away. "It was an accident."

Hank's dad crossed his arms and looked back and forth between Hank and Conner. Then he turned to Slim. "If my boy says it was an accident," he said, "then it was an accident."

"Sorry," said Slim. "I know these kids well, and Conner wouldn't lie." Slim faced Hank. "You're out of the games," he said. "And you're not welcome at Slim's anymore."

"What?" Hank shouted. "That isn't fair! You can't do that!"

"You'll be hearing from my lawyer," Hank's dad growled. Then he grabbed Hank by the elbow again and pulled him towards the exit.

Hannah reached out a hand and helped Conner climb to his feet.

"You can take your ninety seconds again whenever you're ready, Conner," Slim said as he headed back to the judges' table.

"Thanks," Conner said.

"Well, I suppose you were right not to fight," Hannah said. "It all worked out."

Conner watched Hank as his dad dragged him through the crowd. His dad slammed the front doors open and pulled Hank through.

"I guess so," Conner said. "At least now we know why Hank is a bully. He gets it from his dad."

AUTHOR BIO

Eric Stevens lives in Minnesota, USA. He is studying to become a middle-school English teacher. Some of his favourite things include pizza, playing video games, watching cooking shows on TV, riding his bike and trying new restaurants. Some of his least favourite things include olives and shovelling snow.

ILLUSTRATOR BIO

Aburtov has worked in the comic book industry for more than 11 years. In that time, he has illustrated popular characters such as Wolverine, Iron Man, Blade and the Punisher. He lives in Monterrey, Mexico, with his daughter, Ilka, and his beloved wife.

GLOSSARY

accident event that is unfortunate and unplanned

competition contest of some kind

exhausted very tired

extreme exciting and very dangerous

irritated angry or annoyed

menacing threatening or dangerous

routine planned way or pattern of doing something

tournament series of contests in which a number of people try to win the championship

DISCUSSION QUESTIONS

1. Talk about the relationship between Hank and his dad. Do you think Hank can ever stop being a bully?

2. If you were Hannah and Conner, would you have given up the skatepark? Discuss other ways they could have dealt the bullies.

3. Do you think Slim should have done something to stop Hank and his friends? Are there other solutions for dealing with a bully?

WRITING PROMPTS

1. Have you ever had to deal with a bully? Write about what happened and how you resolved things.

2. What was your favourite part of this story? What was your least favourite part? Write a paragraph explaining both choices.

3. Do you think Conner was right to let Hank and his friends get away with their bullying at first? Write about what you would have done.

MORE ABOUT SKATEBOARDING

Skateboarding was invented in the 1950s and is now one of the most popular sports in the world. Skateboarders are always inventing new, more difficult tricks and jumps. Check out these skateboarding-specific terms to learn more:

backside turn or move with your back facing outwards and your toes facing inwards

bailing to leave your skateboard before you crash

carve turn your board at a high speed without sliding on the wheels, usually on a ramp or bank

drop off ride off something involving a drop, like a kerb or a block

fakie riding backwards

goofy standing with your right foot on the front of your skateboard and pushing with your left foot

grind riding along the truck's surface, rather than on the wheels

half-pipe large, U-shaped tube with a flat bottom, usually made of wood but sometimes concrete or metal

heelside side of the board closest to the inside of your heel (right for goofy stance, left for regular)

lip top edge of a ramp or bowl

slamming hard uncontrolled or unexpected fall

vert jump ramp that has a vertical section at the top

THE FUN DOESN'T STOP HERE!